characters created by

lauren child

I've won,

NO I'VE

WON,

No I've won

PUFFIN

Charlie ♥ and ♥ Lola ™

Text based on script written by Dave Ingham

Illustrations from the TV animation produced by Tiger Aspect

PUFFIN BOOKS
Published by the Penguin Group: London, New York, Australia,
Canada, India, Ireland, New Zealand and South Africa
Penguin Books Ltd, Registered Offices: 80 Strand, London WC2R 0RL, England

puffinbooks.com

First published 2005
Published in this edition 2008
1 3 5 7 9 10 8 6 4 2

Made and printed in China
ISBN: 978-0-141-50080-5

I have this little sister Lola.
    She is small and very funny.
    When we play "Who can sit
still the longest!"
        Lola **always** has to win.

Last time we played, Lola said, "I've won!"

I say,
"But I didn't move!"

Lola says,
"Yes you did! I've won!
I always win...
always,
always,
always!"

And then she says,

"I can run faster than a speedy, speedy cheetah, and I can stand on one leg longer than a flamingo!

And I can bounce higher than a bouncy kangaroo, Charlie! See!"

Even when we're **drinking** pink milk,
　　　　　　Lola has to finish first.
　　I say,
"But do you have to **win** at **everything**, Lola?"

　　　　　　And Lola says,

"Yep. I've won!"

So I say,
"How about a **game**
of spoons?"

I know I'm
better than Lola
at the spoon **game**.

But even so,
Lola says, "I'm **winning!**"
I say, "No you're **not!**"
She says, "**I am.**"
I say, "**Not!**"

And then Lola
says,
"Aah, Charlie,
what's **that**?"

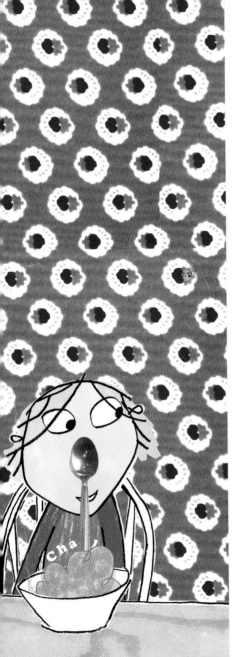

I look up at
the ceiling
and then when
I look back
at Lola...

her spoon has **definitely** moved!
I say,
"Lola, have you... cheated?"
But Lola says,
"Charlie, I've won!"

So then I say,
"Lola, you remember how to play **snap**,
don't you?
You need **two cards** that look the **same**,
then it's a **snap**."

Lola says,
"Yes, **two cards** that look
exactly the **same**,
then it's a
snap."

So I say,
"**five**."

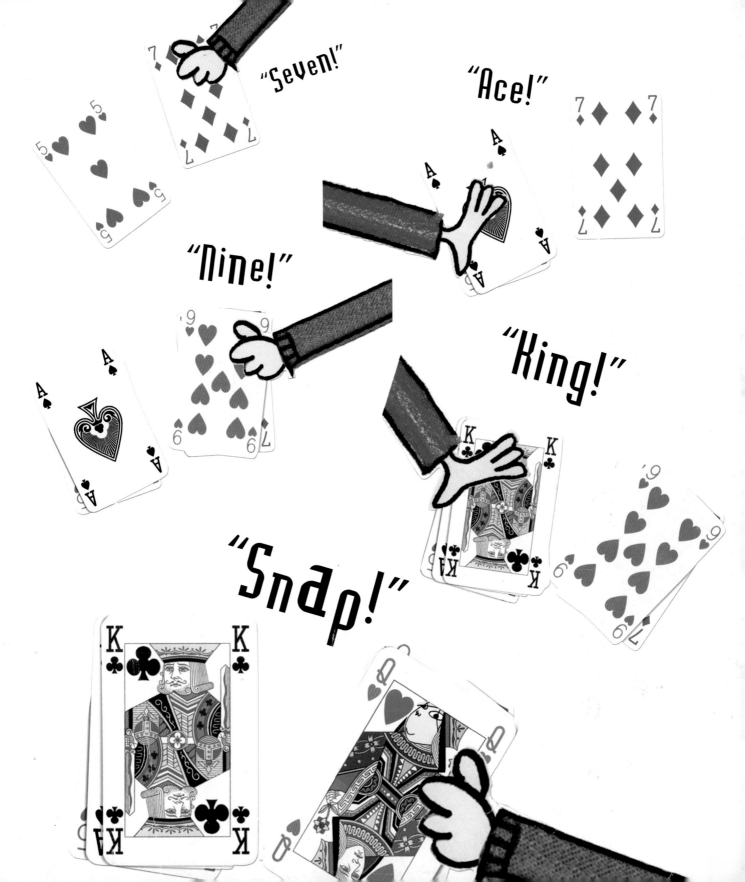

I say, "But they have to be the **same**! And a **queen** is not a **king**!"

Lola says, "But **queens** are married to **kings**. And they both wear **crowns**. And they live in **castles**. So..."

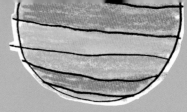

So then I say,
"How about a game of **snakes and ladders?**
You go
up the **ladders**
and
down the **snakes!**
The one who gets to
the **top** is the **winner!**
Do you understand?"

Lola says, "I **do** understand, yes, Charlie!"

I roll first and I shout...

"Six!

1...2...3...4...5...6...

and
up
the
ladder!"

Then it's Lola's turn and she shouts...
"One, two, three! Snake!"

I say,
"Lola, what are you doing?
Snakes are for sliding down.
It's the rules!"

Lola says,

"Charlie, everyone knows snakes aren't all slippy and slidy.

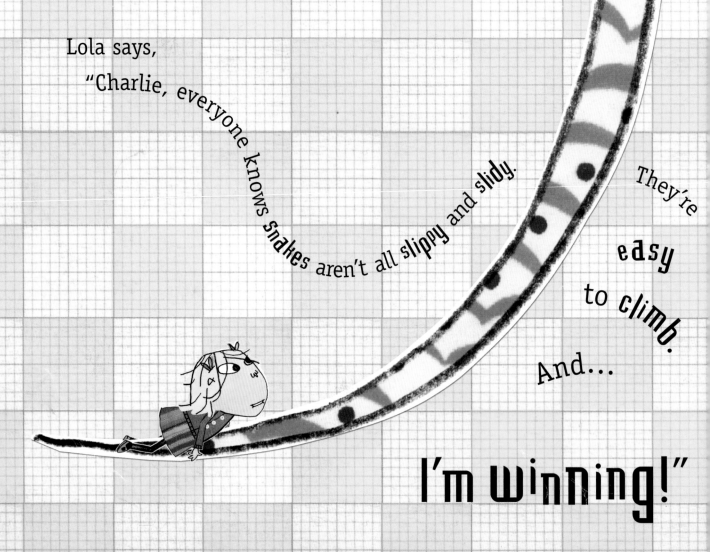

They're easy to climb. And...

I'm winning!"

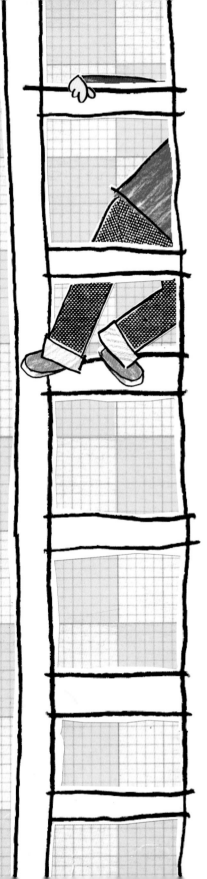

Luckily I get another **six**,
which means **up** a ladder!

But Lola says,
    "Charlie! Dad says you are
not allowed to **climb** a **ladder!**
Not until you are **twenty-three!**"

I say,
"Sorry. **Up** the **ladders**
        and **down** the **snakes.**

That's the rules!"

So Lola shakes the dice and says, "**four!**

1...2...3...4

snake!"

I say, "Bad luck. Now you've got to slide **down** all the way to the bottom.

I've won!"

But guess what?
Lola pretends she's a **snake** charmer

and she charms the **snake** to the finish.

I say,
"But that's
cheating, Lola."

And she says,

"**I've won!**"

So I think of something
that Lola could
    never, never win!

When Dad takes us
        to the park I say,
"How about a race?
        It's once round
    the bendy tree!
Then two big swings
    on the swing!
Down the slide...
    and first one back
to the bench
    is
        the
            winner! OK?"

Lola says,
"But Charlie, I'm only little.
I haven't been on the big slide yet."

And I say,
"Well if you don't want
to win the race, Lola..."

And guess what? I'm actually winning!

"And that's two big swings on the swing!"

But then Lola calls,
"Charlie!
Can
you
help
me?"

And even though
        I'm actually winning,
I say,
"All right, Lola,
    I'm coming!
    Hold on."

We w^h^o^os^h down the slide together.

Lola says,

"Wheeeee-eeee! I'm winning!"

I say,

"Not for long!"

Then I say,
"And the
winner is...
me!

I've
won!
I've won!"

Then I remember Dad saying,
"Charlie, you must give Lola a chance,
because she's so small..."

And I say,
        "Are you all right, Lola?"

And do you know what Lola says?
        She says,

        "That was fun!"

And I say,
"Even though
I won...?"

Lola says,
"Charlie, you don't
have to **win**
all the time,
you know!"

At bedtime, I say,
"Are you **asleep**
           yet, Lola?"

And Lola says,
     "Yes."

     So I say,
"How can you be **asleep**
if you are **talking** to me?"

She says,
     "I'm **sleep-talking!**"

     I say,
"The **first one** to
           fall **asleep** is
the **real winner!**"

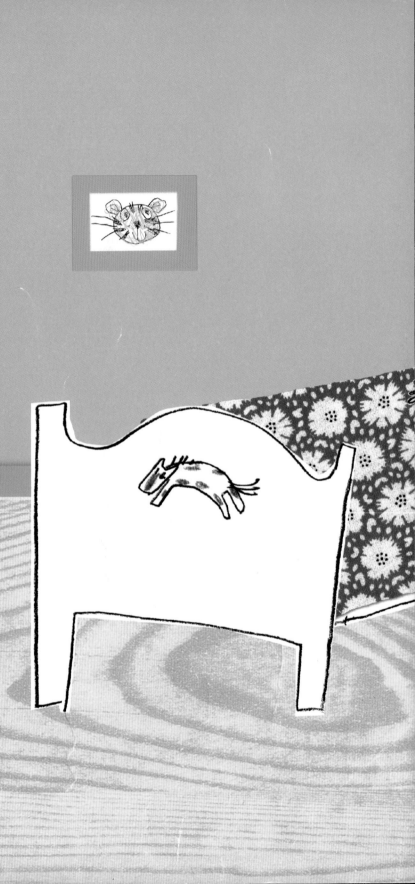

And then Lola whispers, "Charlie? I've won!"
And I say, "No... I've won!"
"I've won!"
"No... I've won!"
"I've won!"